LIONS

BY SUSAN SCHAFER

BENCHMARK BOOKS

MARSHALL CAVENDISH
NEW YORK

Thanks to Paul Severtson, Brooke Love, and John Cheda.

Series consultant:
James Doherty
General Curator
Bronx Zoo, New York

Benchmark Books
Marshall Cavendish Corporation
99 White Plains Road
Tarrytown, NY 10591–9001

Library of Congress Cataloging–in–Publication data:
Schafer, Susan.
Lions/ by Susan Schafer.
p. cm.
Includes bibliographical references and index.
Summary: Describes the physical characteristics, behavior, and habitat of the only large wild cat, other than the American cougar, that is not striped or spotted.
ISBN 0-7614-1166-6
1. Lions–Juvenile literature. [1. Lions.] I. Title
QL737.C23   S287   2000
599.757–dc21   00-024362

Cover photo: *Animals, Animals* / A. & M. Shah

All photographs are used by permission and through the courtesy of *Animals, Animals:*
A. & M. Shah: 5, 15, 19 (bottom), 24, 26, 29, 32, 34, 41; Michael Dick: 7; Norbert Rosing: 11; Zig Leszczynski: 13, 14, 19 (top); S. Osolinski: 17; Leonard Lee Rue III: 20; S. Turner: 23; Hamman/Heldring: 30; Francois Savigny: 35; D. Allen Photography: 37; John Chellman: 38; Len Rue, Jr.: 42; Rick Edwards: 43.

Printed in the United States of America

1 3 5 6 4 2

CONTENTS

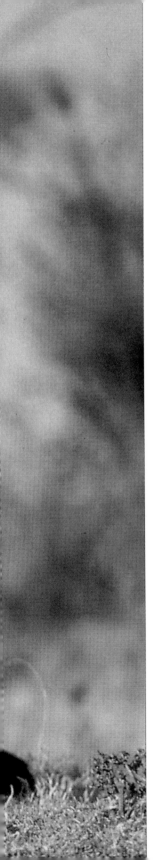

1

INTRODUCING LIONS

Cats live in every part of the world, except for Australia, Antarctica, and many islands. In all, there are thirty-seven *species*, or kinds. But only one —the lion—is known as the king of beasts.

Lions belong to a special group within the cat family called the "big cats." This group also includes tigers, jaguars, leopards, and snow leopards. Only two species of lions survive today: the African lion and its rare cousin the Asian lion.

A MALE AFRICAN LION STANDS GUARD OVER HIS TERRITORY.

The lion is special in many ways. It is the only large wild cat, other than the American cougar that is not spotted or striped. Its fur is a smooth, caramel yellow. It is also the only cat that lives in a group, called a *pride*. The pride works as a team to hunt for food and protect the family.

Lions are also unique in another way: males and females don't look alike. Unlike females, adult males have a long, furry mane around their neck. And the lion is the only cat with a tuft of black hair at the tip of its tail.

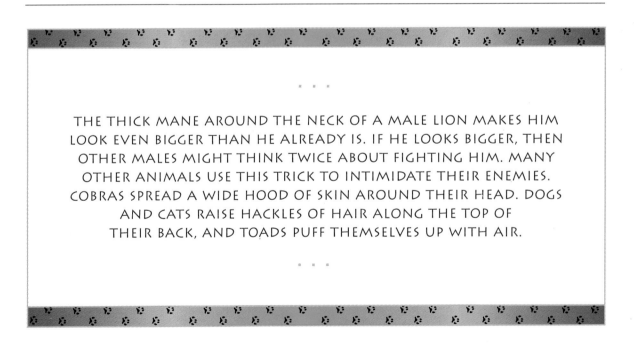

THE THICK MANE AROUND THE NECK OF A MALE LION MAKES HIM LOOK EVEN BIGGER THAN HE ALREADY IS. IF HE LOOKS BIGGER, THEN OTHER MALES MIGHT THINK TWICE ABOUT FIGHTING HIM. MANY OTHER ANIMALS USE THIS TRICK TO INTIMIDATE THEIR ENEMIES. COBRAS SPREAD A WIDE HOOD OF SKIN AROUND THEIR HEAD. DOGS AND CATS RAISE HACKLES OF HAIR ALONG THE TOP OF THEIR BACK, AND TOADS PUFF THEMSELVES UP WITH AIR.

THE SNOW LEOPARD, A DISTANT RELATIVE OF THE LION, LIVES IN CENTRAL ASIA.

Only the tiger is larger than the lion. Measuring from the tip of its nose to the tip of its tail, a male lion can be over 9 feet (2.8 meters) long. That's as long as a small car. Lions are tall, too. Male lions may reach 3.5 feet (1 meter) at the shoulder.

MALE LIONS ARE LARGER THAN LIONESSES. THEY ALSO HAVE A LARGE TUFT OF FUR, CALLED A MANE, AROUND THEIR NECK.

THIS IS THE SKELETON OF A LION.

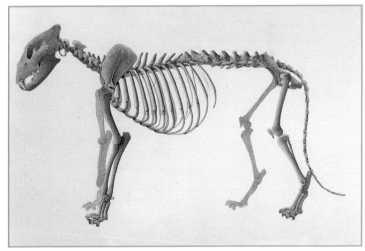

A LION MAY ONLY REACH THE WAIST OF A FULL-GROWN HUMAN BEING, BUT IT IS MUCH MORE POWERFUL.

Males weigh 400 to 500 pounds (180–225 kilograms), far more than the biggest professional football players. The females, called lionesses, are a trim 275 to 300 pounds (125–135 kilograms). Still, that's probably more than three or four of you put together. Whatever their size, lions are strong and muscular with broad heads, huge jaws, powerful legs, and sharp teeth and claws. They are built for hunting on the wide grassy plains.

The heaviest wild lion ever was a male that weighed about 690 pounds (312 kg). Most wild males don't weigh more than 400 pounds (181 kg). Lions in zoos, however, are often much heavier than lions in the wild. That's because they get plenty of food but not as much exercise. Wild lions have to walk for miles to find food, and then they have to catch it!

A PRIDE LOOKS FOR PREY.

2

PRIDES OF THE PLAINS

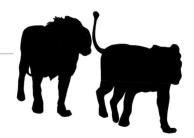

A dry wind blows across the African savanna—home to the largest population of lions in the world. A *savanna* is a special kind of grassland. It has a short rainy season and a long dry season. Only thorny acacia trees manage to pop up here and there, reaching their spindly branches toward the sky. Otherwise, the savanna is a sea of grass as far as the eye can see.

The African savanna, south of the Sahara Desert, is rich in life. It is home to more kinds of grazing animals than

THE AFRICAN SAVANNA, SHOWN HERE IN KENYA, IS VERY GREEN AFTER THE RAINY SEASON.

LIONS PROWL THE SAVANNA IN SEARCH OF PREY DURING THE DRY SEASON.

anywhere else on Earth. Zebra, gazelle, topi, wildebeest, impala, eland, warthog, and buffalo feed all day long on the savanna's grasses. Where there are grazing animals, lions cannot be far away. Lions are *predators;* they feed on other animals.

IMPALAS ARE ONE OF THE HERD ANIMALS LIONS FEED ON.

LIONS LIKE TO CUDDLE. THEY OFTEN REST WITH A HEAD OR PAW ON ANOTHER LION. WHEN MEETING, THEY RUB AGAINST EACH OTHER'S CHEEKS OR BODIES. THIS RUBBING CREATES BONDS AMONG LIONS. IT SHOWS THAT THEY ARE AT PEACE AND THAT THEY RECOGNIZE THE POSITION OF OTHER LIONS WITHIN THE PRIDE. THEY ALSO GROOM THEMSELVES AND EACH OTHER TO KEEP THEIR FUR CLEAN. TINY HOOKLIKE BUMPS ON THE TOP OF THEIR TONGUES MAKE EXCELLENT SCRUB BRUSHES.

Lions travel many miles in search of food, water, and shade. They roam the scrublands and sparse forests around the savanna, but they prefer the grassland because there they can see farther to hunt. Each pride has its own special area called a *territory*. The territory might be small if there is plenty of food or large if food is scarce. Sometimes a pride will cross another pride's territory in search of food.

Male lions defend their territory from other males by roaring loudly. They mark their territory by spraying their urine on trees and rocks. If their warnings are ignored, they will attack.

A pride of lions may have up to five males and fifteen females, not counting cubs. Only one male, however, will be the *dominant* lion. The dominant lion takes the lead in defending the pride. The others support him. Males are usually closely related to each other, but not to the females in the pride. The females are also closely related. Mothers, daughters, sisters, and aunts all live together.

Each lion in the pride has a special job. The job of the males is to protect the pride. Males are huskier than

A LIONESS PREPARING TO TAKE A DRINK
AT THE KALAHARI GEMSBOK PARK IN
SOUTH AFRICA. DURING THE DRY SEASON,
WATER IS SCARCE, AND LIONS MAY HAVE
TO TRAVEL MILES TO FIND A WATER HOLE
SUCH AS THIS ONE.

females. They are built for fighting. The lionesses do most of the hunting. They are slimmer, so they can move quickly when catching prey.

Hyenas look like dogs, but they are actually more closely related to cats. Hyenas are not only scavengers but also talented hunters. Like lions, they hunt in groups. Sometimes lions become the scavengers and chase the hyenas from their kills.

(OPPOSITE TOP) A LOUD ROAR WARNS OTHER LIONS TO STAY AWAY.

(OPPOSITE BOTTOM) A DOMINANT LION KEEPS WATCH FOR PREDATORS WHO WOULD ATTACK AND KILL THE CUBS IN HIS PRIDE.

3
TEAMS ON THE HUNT

Creeping forward, a lioness moves silently through the grass. At the edge of a clearing, she drops to her belly and holds perfectly still. Her golden fur blends with the dry grass. Patiently she waits, keeping her eyes on a group of wildebeest and zebras.

On the far side of the clearing, five more lionesses walk into view. They walk side by side, spread out in a row. They are teammates of the hiding lioness. By working together on the hunt, they can catch *prey* much larger than themselves. Farther behind, the male lions wait, watching over the cubs.

The zebras see the five lionesses and begin barking like startled dogs. Their nervous bark warns others to beware. Hearing the warning, the wildebeests

(OPPOSITE) THIS LIONESS IS STALKING PREY. THE TALL BROWN GRASS OF THE SAVANNA CAMOUFLAGES HER.

move away. The zebras follow, but the herds are now walking straight toward the lioness hiding in the grass. They can't see or smell her. She is hiding downwind so the breeze can't blow her smell toward the herds and warn them.

Suddenly, the five lionesses rush the herds. The wildebeests and zebras leap forward, sensing the attack is from the rear. One wildebeest, slower than the rest, weaves toward the hidden lioness. In a flash, she leaps

Lions are not speedsters. Most of their prey can outrun them. Wildebeests, zebras, and other herd animals can run faster than 45 miles (72 km) per hour. The top speed for a lion is only about 35 miles (56 km) per hour. Lions must hide or sneak up on their prey and use a short burst of speed to catch them. In comparison, cheetahs, the fastest land animal, can race at up to 70 miles (112 km) per hour.

A LIONESS RUSHING TOWARD HER PREY. SINCE LIONS ARE NOT FAST ANIMALS, THEY MUST GET AS CLOSE AS THEY CAN TO THEIR PREY BEFORE ATTACKING.

THIS LIONESS IS CHASING A
HERD OF WILDEBEESTS.

LIONS OFTEN PURSUE PREY THAT IS MUCH LARGER THAN THEY ARE. ALL OF THE LIONESSES IN THIS PRIDE ARE NEEDED TO BRING DOWN A CAPE BUFFALO.

from the grass. If she can knock the wildebeest to the ground, the other females will soon catch up to help.

The lioness grabs for the wildebeest's neck but misses and barely catches a leg. The wildebeest kicks wildly and breaks away, fleeing onto the savanna.

26

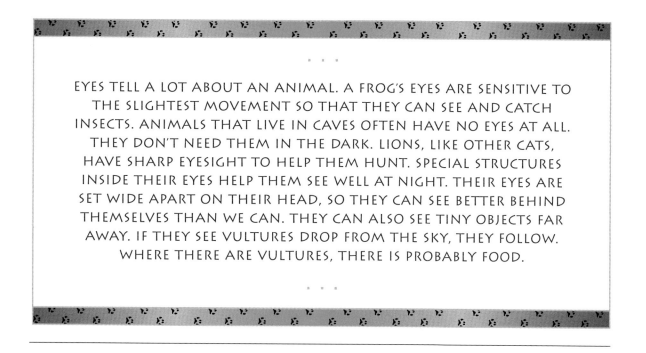

EYES TELL A LOT ABOUT AN ANIMAL. A FROG'S EYES ARE SENSITIVE TO THE SLIGHTEST MOVEMENT SO THAT THEY CAN SEE AND CATCH INSECTS. ANIMALS THAT LIVE IN CAVES OFTEN HAVE NO EYES AT ALL. THEY DON'T NEED THEM IN THE DARK. LIONS, LIKE OTHER CATS, HAVE SHARP EYESIGHT TO HELP THEM HUNT. SPECIAL STRUCTURES INSIDE THEIR EYES HELP THEM SEE WELL AT NIGHT. THEIR EYES ARE SET WIDE APART ON THEIR HEAD, SO THEY CAN SEE BETTER BEHIND THEMSELVES THAN WE CAN. THEY CAN ALSO SEE TINY OBJECTS FAR AWAY. IF THEY SEE VULTURES DROP FROM THE SKY, THEY FOLLOW. WHERE THERE ARE VULTURES, THERE IS PROBABLY FOOD.

The lioness won't follow. She will save her energy. Lions rely on ambush, not running, to catch their prey. The hunters will try again somewhere else.

Lions must hunt nearly every day or night, because they miss more animals than they catch. Those they catch are usually young, weak, sick, or old. If they can, they will steal food from other predators like the hyena or cheetah. Sometimes lions do not find anything to eat for two or three days. Lions spend most of their time sleeping—up to twenty-two hours a day. Sleeping helps conserve energy for hunting.

When feeding, lions hiss, snarl, and fight among themselves. Each tries to eat as much as it can. A male lion might gulp down 90 pounds (40 kilograms) of food at a meal. That would be like eating 360 quarter–pound hamburgers!

As the lions feed, their cubs wait impatiently for leftovers. If they move in too soon, they might get hurt. Although males sometimes share food, females almost never do, even with their own cubs. This is one of the few times they don't cooperate.

After feeding, peace returns to the pride. Settling down, the lions yawn lazily. They groom themselves and each other, licking away the mess from their faces and paws. The fierce hunters look like contented kittens.

AFTER EATING THEIR HUGE MEAL,
LIONS LICK ONE ANOTHER CLEAN
AND SETTLE DOWN FOR A LONG NAP.

4
A LION'S LIFE

A lioness is restless. First she paces back and forth. Then she rolls on the ground. Almost immediately she leaps up and trots toward the dominant lion of her pride. Abruptly she turns, walks away, and rolls on the ground again.

The lion follows her, but as he tries to lick her, she snarls at him and jumps away. A minute later she is back, plopping herself down in front of him. When she is ready, the pair will *mate*.

About three months later, she leaves the pride to have her young. Finding a special hiding place in the brush or among some rocks, she gives birth to

A PAIR OF LIONS IN THE KALAHARI DESERT, IN BOTSWANA, PREPARES TO MATE.

WHEN COURTING, LIONS OFTEN SNUGGLE CLOSE TO EACH OTHER.

two or three cubs. Each *cub* weighs about 3 pounds (1.5 kilograms). She cares for them on her own, leaving only to drink and hunt for food. Until she takes them back to the pride, she will not have the help of other lions.

In her hiding place, she nurses and cleans her young. Within the first week or two, the cubs open their eyes. Shortly after, they walk. For safety, the lioness might move her young. Picking them up in her mouth, she takes them one at a time to a new hiding place.

By the time they are a month old, the cubs are bouncing around and playing. But they never venture far from their hiding place. With their mother gone for hours at a time, they might need to dash for safety if danger threatens.

At about two months, the cubs are old enough to join the pride. Most lionesses seem to have their cubs at about the same time, so when they return to the pride, all of the young are roughly the same age. Now the females help each other care for the cubs.

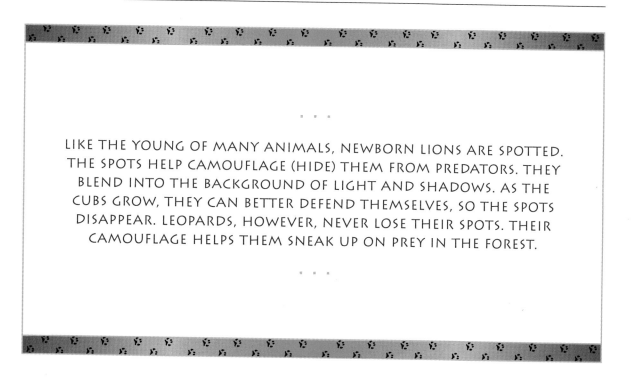

LIKE THE YOUNG OF MANY ANIMALS, NEWBORN LIONS ARE SPOTTED. THE SPOTS HELP CAMOUFLAGE (HIDE) THEM FROM PREDATORS. THEY BLEND INTO THE BACKGROUND OF LIGHT AND SHADOWS. AS THE CUBS GROW, THEY CAN BETTER DEFEND THEMSELVES, SO THE SPOTS DISAPPEAR. LEOPARDS, HOWEVER, NEVER LOSE THEIR SPOTS. THEIR CAMOUFLAGE HELPS THEM SNEAK UP ON PREY IN THE FOREST.

At six months, the cubs are about a quarter the size of the adults. They won't take part in a hunt until they are over a year old, but they practice hunting every day by playing. They stalk the adults' tails. Pouncing on one another, they wrestle and pretend to bite. They leap at twigs in ponds and attack blowing leaves. They also learn by watching the lionesses hunt. After two or three years, the cubs are ready to live on their own. Females stay with the pride until they are too old to keep up or claim a piece of the pride's kill. They usually live longer than males, up to eighteen years.

A LION CUB SHORTLY AFTER IT HAS JOINED THE PRIDE. NOTICE THE MALE LION IN THE BACKGROUND. HE IS KEEPING WATCH OVER THE CUBS TO MAKE SURE NO PREDATORS SNATCH THEM AWAY.

THESE YOUNG LIONS ARE PRACTICING THEIR HUNTING AND FIGHTING
SKILLS BY PLAYING WITH EACH OTHER.

Young males are chased away. Joining their brothers or cousins, they form small bachelor groups and roam the plains. When they are strong enough, they fight for a pride of their own. It won't be easy. Even if they succeed, they will last only a few years before younger, stronger males steal the pride from them.

When an old male lion loses his pride, he becomes a wanderer once again. Large animals are hard to catch, so he hunts smaller game like hares. He will never return to his pride. Slowly he loses weight as his strength and teeth wear out.

The male lions in a pride will defend the pride against strange males, but they do not often fight one another. The males need to stick together, since a group of males is better able to protect a pride than a single male.

A LION CANNOT BE THE LEADER OF A PRIDE FOREVER. SOMEDAY, A YOUNGER LION OR GROUP OF LIONS WILL TAKE HIS PLACE, AND HE WILL BECOME A WANDERER AGAIN.

At most, he will live about fourteen years. The king is at the end of his time, but somewhere his young sons are starting new prides of their own. Somewhere his grandchildren are being born. The cycle of his life goes on.

37

5
DISAPPEARING SAVANNA

Lions once roamed Africa, Southern Europe, the Middle East, and Asia. Then people began to kill them. Asian lions nearly disappeared. In 1913, only twenty remained. Now they live in a small reserve in western India and their numbers are slowly increasing. Still, they are an endangered species. The African lion has fared slightly better. It is not *endangered* yet, but it is *vulnerable*. It survives in national parks, game reserves, and zoos.

People have harmed the lion and its *habitat*. They build houses and farms where lions live. They use the land to graze *domestic* animals, such as cattle. The cattle eat the grass that wild herd animals need to survive. Without these herd animals, lions have no food. If hungry lions then kill cattle, people get angry and kill the lions. Cattle and other domestic animals,

THE HABITAT OF LIONS HAS GREATLY DECREASED OVER THE LAST HUNDRED YEARS.

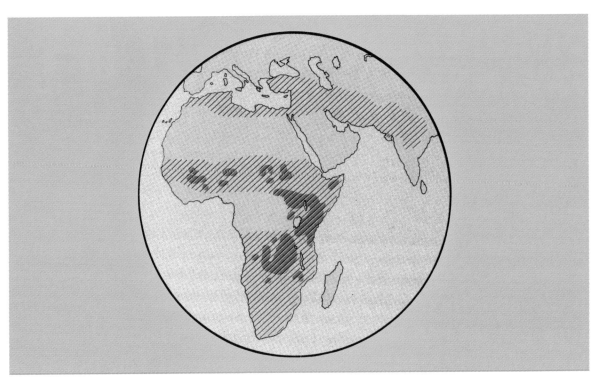

WHERE LIONS LIVE

PAST HABITAT

PRESENT HABITAT

Lions once roamed much of Africa, the Middle East, and Asia. The African lion's habitat is much smaller now. The Asian lion is found in only a small area within India.

ASIAN LIONS, SUCH AS THIS ONE IN INDIA, ARE AN ENDANGERED SPECIES.

such as dogs, also spread diseases. A disease called *distemper* recently killed a third of the lions in Serengeti National Park in East Africa. On top of that, people still hunt lions for sport. They want to hang a lion's skin or a stuffed lion's head in their homes.

Many people, however, want to save the savanna and the lions that live there. They work to stop the spread of disease and to educate people about saving wild animals. Park rangers try to stop *poachers*. Scientists study the lions. The more they learn, the more they can do to help.

CATTLE AND OTHER DOMESTIC ANIMALS HAVE REPLACED SOME OF THE HERD ANIMALS THAT LIONS ONCE HUNTED THROUGHOUT AFRICA.

HAVE YOU EVER HEARD OF A LIGER? IT IS A CROSS BETWEEN A MALE LION AND A FEMALE TIGER. HOW ABOUT A TIGON? IT IS A CROSS BETWEEN A MALE TIGER AND A FEMALE LION. THIS SHOWS HOW CLOSELY RELATED THE LION IS TO THE TIGER. PEOPLE HAVE BRED LIGERS FOR OVER A HUNDRED YEARS. THEY EVEN CROSSED A LION WITH A TIGON TO GET A LITIGON! IT LIVED IN A ZOO IN INDIA AND WEIGHED 800 POUNDS (363 KG).

By working together, people can save the prides of Africa. Only then will the lion—with its head held high and its golden eyes staring across the savanna—continue to rule as king of the animals.

EVEN THOUGH AFRICAN LIONS ARE NOT ENDANGERED, HUMAN POPULATIONS MOVING ONTO THE SAVANNA HAVE AN IMPACT ON THEIR LIVES.

cub: the young of certain animals, such as a lion or bear.

domestic: not wild; tame; grown for use by people.

dominant: the most important or most powerful individual in a group.

endangered: an animal or plant at risk of becoming extinct, or dying off forever.

habitat: the place where an animal or plant is normally found.

mate: when a male and female join as a pair in order to produce young.

poacher: a person who hunts or fishes illegally.

predator: an animal that lives by killing and eating other animals.

prey: an animal hunted for food by another animal. Lions prey on Zebras.

pride: a group of lions that lives together.

savanna: an open grassland with scattered trees or shrubs.

species: a kind of plant or animal. A lion is a species of cat.

territory: a particular area chosen by an animal or group of animals as its own.

vulnerable: likely to be hurt or destroyed.

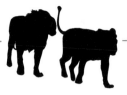

BOOKS

Curry–Lindahl, Kai. *Wildlife of the Prairies and Plains.* New York: Abrams, 1981.

Harman, Amanda. *Lions.* Tarrytown, NY: Marshall Cavendish, 1997.

Morris, Desmond. *Cat World: A Feline Encyclopedia.* New York: Penguin, 1997.

National Geographic Book of Mammals, Volume Two. Washington, DC: National Geographic Society, 1981.

Simon, Seymour. *Big Cats.* New York: Harper Collins, 1991.

The Way Nature Works. New York: Macmillan, 1992.

F I N D O U T M O R E

WEBSITES

The Asiatic Lion Information Center
http://wkweb4.cableinet.co.uk/alic

Lions and Tigers Appeal (the Edinburgh Zoo)
http://www.lionsandtigers.scotland.net/flash/front.htm

Lion Research Center
http://www.lionresearch.org

The Kingdom of Lions
http://home.worldonline.nl/~rlion/lkindex.htm

Susan Schafer is a writer and science teacher who enjoys sharing her love for animals with others. She has written a number of books about animals, including *Turtles* and *Lizards* in the Marshall Cavendish *Perfect Pets* series. She lives on a ranch outside of San Luis Obispo, California, where she is occasionally blessed with the sighting of a mountain lion.